In My Backyard

By Valarie Giogas
Illustrated by Katherine Zecca

To the men in my life, CG, JAG and RDG—VG
To my sister, Cyndi—KZ

Thanks to Sherry Crawley,
Director of Education at Zoo Atlanta
and to Helen Fischel,
Associate Director of Education at the Delaware Nature Society
for verifying the accuracy of the information in the book.
And thanks to Caryl Widdowson
of Safe & Sound Wildlife Rehabilitation (ME) for her help.

In my backyard I can see
   groups of baby animals
   all around me.
They creep, they crawl, they run, and hide.
They munch, they crunch, they sleep outside.

In my backyard I can see
　　one doe's fawn
　　peeking at me.
He sees me through the leaves and brush,
　　then runs to mama in a rush.

1

In my backyard I can see
a prickle of two pups
grunting at me.
They gnaw on rusty hoes and rakes,
then chew on twigs and tree bark flakes.

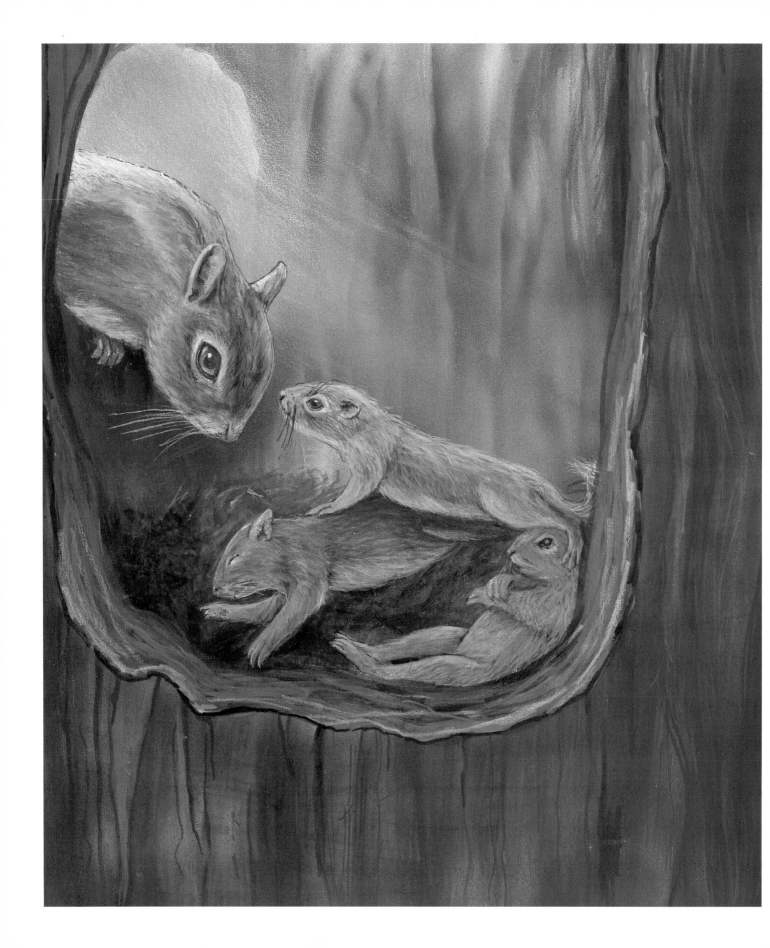

3

In my backyard I can see
   a scurry of three pups
   gazing at me.
It's very crowded in their nest
   which makes it really hard to rest.

4

In my backyard I can see
   a nursery of four cubs
   spying on me.
At night they search inside our trash.
I always hear the barrels crash.

In my backyard I can see
    a nest of five bunnies
    twitching at me.
They've gotten through the garden gate.
Just look at all the plants they ate!

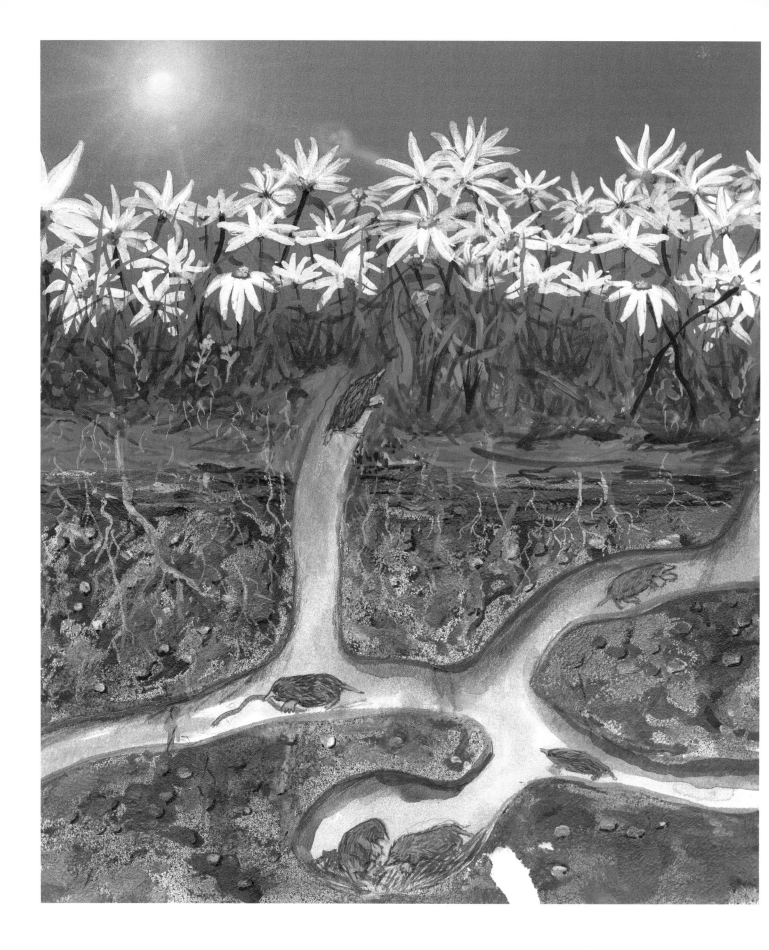

In my backyard I can see
a labor of six pups
running from me.
They cannot see their lunch of worms,
but they can hear them as they squirm.

7

In my backyard I can see
   a surfeit of seven kits
   squinting at me.
They hunt for grubs and ants and snails,
   and sometimes eat the eggs of quails.

8

In my backyard I can see
a pit of eight hatchlings
slithering near me.
They twist amongst the leaves and vines
and blend into a swirled design.

In my backyard I can see
a skulk of nine pups
sleeping near me.
They cuddle in their den all day,
then late at night they look for prey.

10

In my backyard I can see
a swarm of ten nymphs
chirping at me.
They listen to their mother's sound
and munch on leaves that they have found.

For Creative Minds

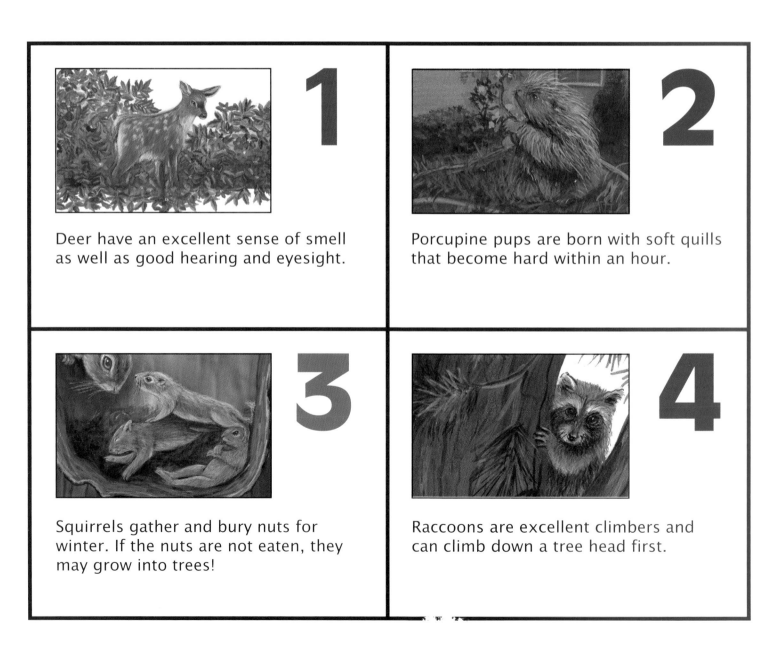

1

Deer have an excellent sense of smell as well as good hearing and eyesight.

2

Porcupine pups are born with soft quills that become hard within an hour.

3

Squirrels gather and bury nuts for winter. If the nuts are not eaten, they may grow into trees!

4

Raccoons are excellent climbers and can climb down a tree head first.

Rabbits "talk" to each other through smell and touch.

Moles have bad eyesight, but they can hear insects from a distance and have a good sense of smell.

Skunks are only born in the spring. The kits are almost blind and don't have fur.

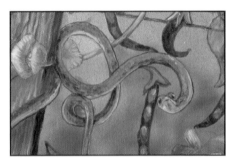

Snakes that are born alive are called snakelets. If they come from eggs, they are called hatchlings. They smell by flicking their tongues in and out.

Foxes are good tree climbers. Many are good swimmers and can run up to twenty miles per hour.

Grasshopper nymphs look like little adult grasshoppers without wings.

1 a fawn is a
baby deer

2 pups are baby
porcupines

3 pups are
baby squirrels

4 cubs are
baby raccoons

5 bunnies are
baby rabbits

6 pups are
baby moles

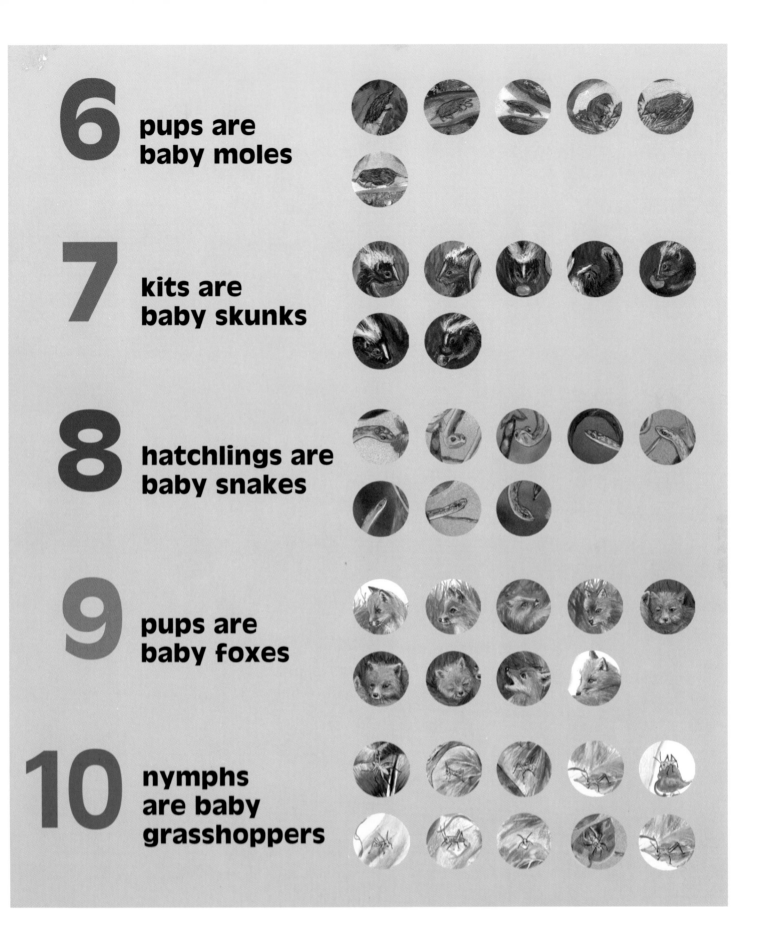

7 kits are
baby skunks

8 hatchlings are
baby snakes

9 pups are
baby foxes

10 nymphs
are baby
grasshoppers

Animal Signs All Around You

Animals leave "signs" that show they were there. Find a nature spot: your backyard, a park, or a nature center. See how many "animal signs" you can find. Here are just a few:

scat (poop)

pieces of homes
(bird nests, spider webs, etc.)

broken or chewed plants

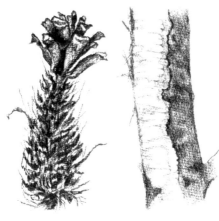

chewed pinecones, nuts
or tree bark

tracks

feathers, shells, or bones

Caring For Wildlife Around You

Some or all of the animals mentioned in this book may live or pass through your yard, even if you never see them! What can you do to protect wild animals?

- Keep pets inside.
- Please pick up your trash—especially plastic. Wild animals may eat the trash and get sick.
- Don't touch any wild animals; they are just that—wild!
- Don't try to keep them or to make them pets.
- Feed and watch birds but don't feed other wild animals.

What to Do If You Find an Injured Animal

Wildlife rehabilitators are people who care for injured wild animals and nurse them back to health. It is always a good idea to look up and find a wildlife rehabilitator in your area before you need one! Check online, look in the phone book, or ask a veterinarian.

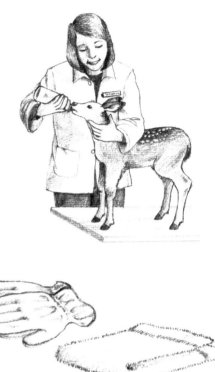

If the animal is alert and big enough to harm you, call the wildlife rehabilitator or your local animal control. Let professionals help the animal.

If the animal is small, of no danger to you, and looks like it may be nursed back to health, try to get it to a rehabilitator:

- Wear gloves or wrap the animal in a towel so that you don't touch it. Remember that the animal, if conscious, will be scared and may try to claw or bite. An unconscious animal could wake up any time.

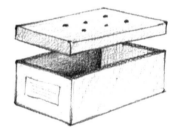

- If it is cold, place a heating pad on low or a ziplock bag of very warm water in part of a box (so the animal can move away from the heat if necessary) and put a towel or blanket on top of the heat source. Place the injured animal on top of the warm side, on top of the towel or blanket.

- Tightly cover the box, but please make sure that there are ventilation holes for the animal to breathe.

- Do NOT try to feed the animal.

- If you think an animal is orphaned, leave it alone until you are positive that the mother is not returning. It is normal for animal parents to leave to get food, sometimes for several hours or even all day. If, however, you know that the mother is dead, call a wildlife rehabilitator or wildlife expert to get the animal.

Giogas, Valarie.
In my backyard / by Valarie Giogas ; illustrated by Katherine Zecca.

p. : col. ill. ; cm.

Includes "For Creative Minds" section with animal facts
memory game and information on caring for wildlife.
ISBN-13: 978-0-9777423-1-8 (hardcover)
ISBN-10: 978-1-9343591-7-4 (pbk.)

1. Animals--Infancy--Juvenile literature. 2. Counting--Juvenile
literature. 3. Animals--Infancy. 4. Counting. 5. Stories in rhyme.
I. Zecca, Katherine. II. Title.

QL751.5 .G56 2007
591.5   2006940900

Printed in Malaysia

Sylvan Dell Publishing
976 Houston Northcutt Blvd., Suite 3
Mt. Pleasant, SC 29464